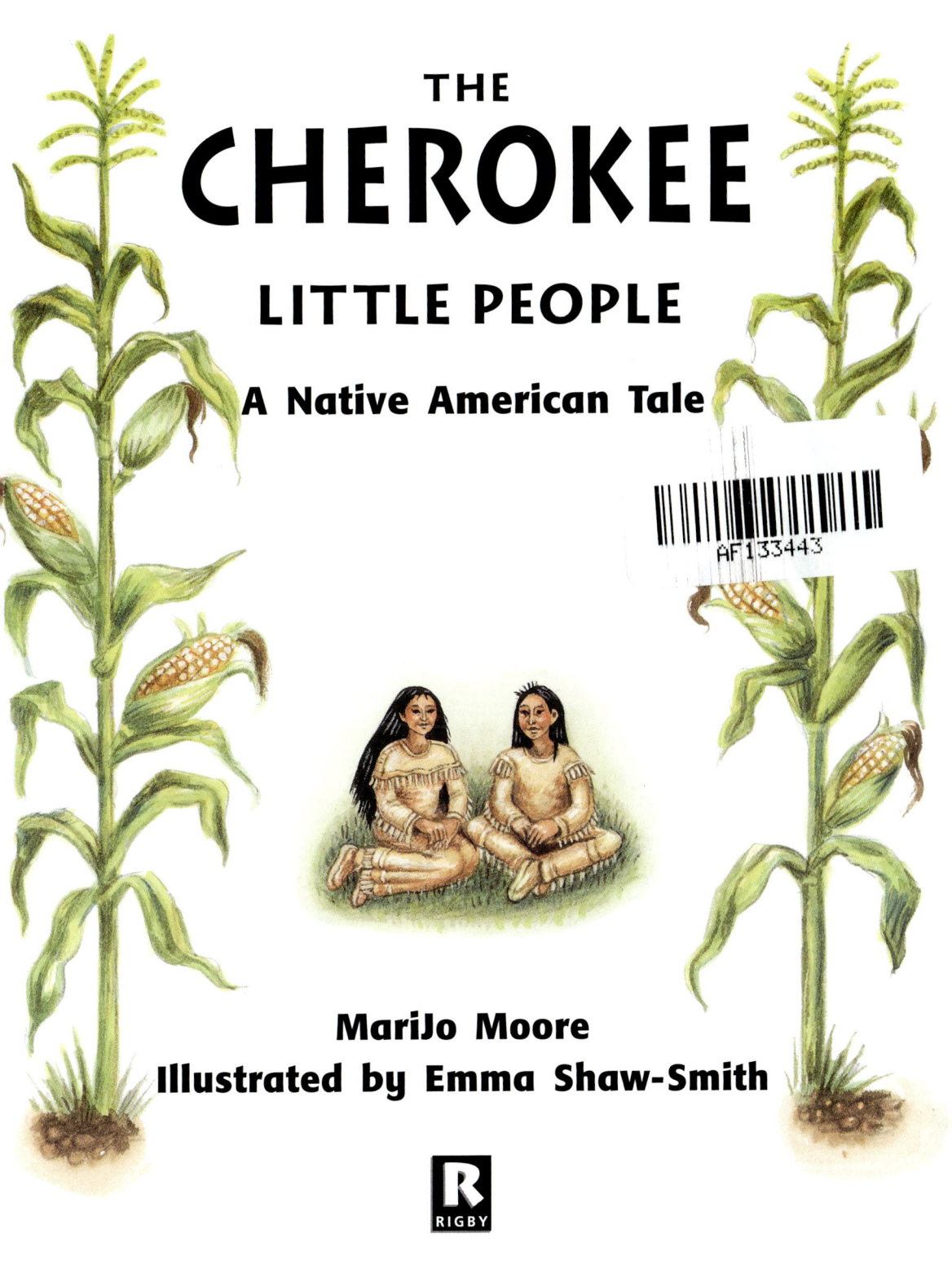

THE CHEROKEE LITTLE PEOPLE

A Native American Tale

MariJo Moore
Illustrated by Emma Shaw-Smith

RIGBY

There once lived a Cherokee man and
woman named Tooni and Polly.
They lived in a little cabin
in the mountains.

Every spring they planted corn.

In summer the corn grew and grew.

In fall Polly and Tooni gathered the corn.

In the long cold winter,
they made food from the corn.

One year the corn grew and grew and grew.
There was so much corn that
Tooni and Polly couldn't gather it all.
"I will go into town and try to get help,"
said Tooni, and off he went.

Tooni was gone for a long time.
Polly waited and waited.
She saw many crows in the sky.
She began to worry.
"If Tooni doesn't come back soon,
the crows will eat all the corn," said Polly.
Polly began to cry.

Two Cherokee Little People,
Kamama and Kanunu,
were playing in the big tree
next to the little cabin.
They heard Polly crying.

Kamama and Kanunu peeped from the tree.
They saw Polly crying.
They saw all the corn.
They saw the crows flying over the corn.
At once, Kamama and Kanunu knew what was wrong.

Kamama and Kanunu danced and sang a special song to make Polly go to sleep.

Then Kamama and Kanunu
and their friends
gathered the corn.
They put the corn
next to the little cabin.

The next morning, Tooni came home. He hadn't found any helpers because everyone was busy in their own fields. He looked at the empty cornfield. "Who has gathered all the corn?" he wondered.

"Wake up, Polly," said Tooni.
"Did you gather all the corn?"
"No, I didn't gather all the corn," said Polly.
"I have been asleep. I had a dream.
I dreamed that the Cherokee Little People
gathered the corn."

Then Polly and Tooni saw the corn
next to the cabin.
They saw little footprints on the porch.
At once they knew that
the Cherokee Little People
had gathered the corn.

Polly made many pairs of small moccasins.
Tooni made cornbread from the corn.
He cut the cornbread into tiny pieces.

Tooni took the pieces of cornbread and
the little moccasins and
put them under the big tree.

When night came, the Cherokee Little People ate the cornbread.
They put on their new moccasins and danced by the light of the moon.

Tooni and Polly gave the gifts to say "thank you" to the Cherokee Little People for helping them.
That is the Cherokee way.